A fine song I have made
To please you, my dear;
And if it's well sung,
'Twill be charming to hear.

The piano arrangements, by Eddie Graf, have been created for intermediate pianists, whatever their age. They are simple, yet imaginative and wonderfully fun to play.

A note to guitarists and other chordal people: the guitar chords indicated grew out of the piano arrangements. Where the changes are too rapid or complex, feel free to adapt them to your abilities and taste. Chords in parentheses can be omitted.

Acknowledgements

Boundless thanks for guiding this whole project go to Molly Thom, our resident amanuensis and to Patsy Aldana, the most patient and skillful of editors. We are grateful to the following for granting permission to include copyrighted material in this collection: "I've Got Rings on My Fingers," copyright © 1909 Francis, Day & Hunter and renewed by Warner Bros., Inc., publisher and owner of all rights for the United States and Canada, all rights reserved, used by permission. "Where's My Pajamas," by Pete Seeger copyright © 1985 by Stormking Music Inc., all rights reserved, used by permission. "My Pony Boy," by Bobby Heath and Charlie O'Donnell, printed by permission of the copyright owner, Jerry Vogel Music Company, Inc., 501 Fifth Avenue, New York, N.Y. 10017. "One for Me and One for You," and "One, One, Cinnamon Bun," by Clyde Watson, reprinted by permission of Philomel Books from CATCH ME AND KISS ME AND SAY IT AGAIN, text copyrighted © 1978 by Clyde Watson. "Go to Sleep Now My Pumpkin," from a German folk tune "Kommt ein Vogel geflogen," words by Pat Carfra from a song by Lou McNamee from the record SONGS FOR SLEEPYHEADS AND OUT-OF-BEDS!, used by permission from A & M Records. "Baby Bye Here's a Fly," from a German folk tune, Hänschen Klein.

Third printing 1989
All rights reserved.
Douglas & McIntyre Ltd., 1615 Venables Street, Vancouver, British Columbia V5L 2H1

Canadian Cataloguing in Publication Data

Mother Goose.
  Sharon, Lois and Bram's Mother Goose

Includes music.
ISBN 0-88894-487-X

1. Nursery rhymes, English. 2. Children's songs. 3. Children's poetry, English. I. Sharon, Lois and Bram. II. Kovalski, Maryann. III. Title.

M1990.M68S42   1985   j784.6'2405   C85-098850-0

Cover photograph by Gordon Hay
Design by Michael Solomon
Printed in Hong Kong
by Everbest Printing Co., Ltd.

SHARON, LOIS & BRAM'S
MOTHER GOOSE

★

Illustrated by
MARYANN KOVALSKI

Three elephants went out to play

DOUGLAS & McINTYRE
Vancouver and Toronto

Upon a spider's web one day . . .

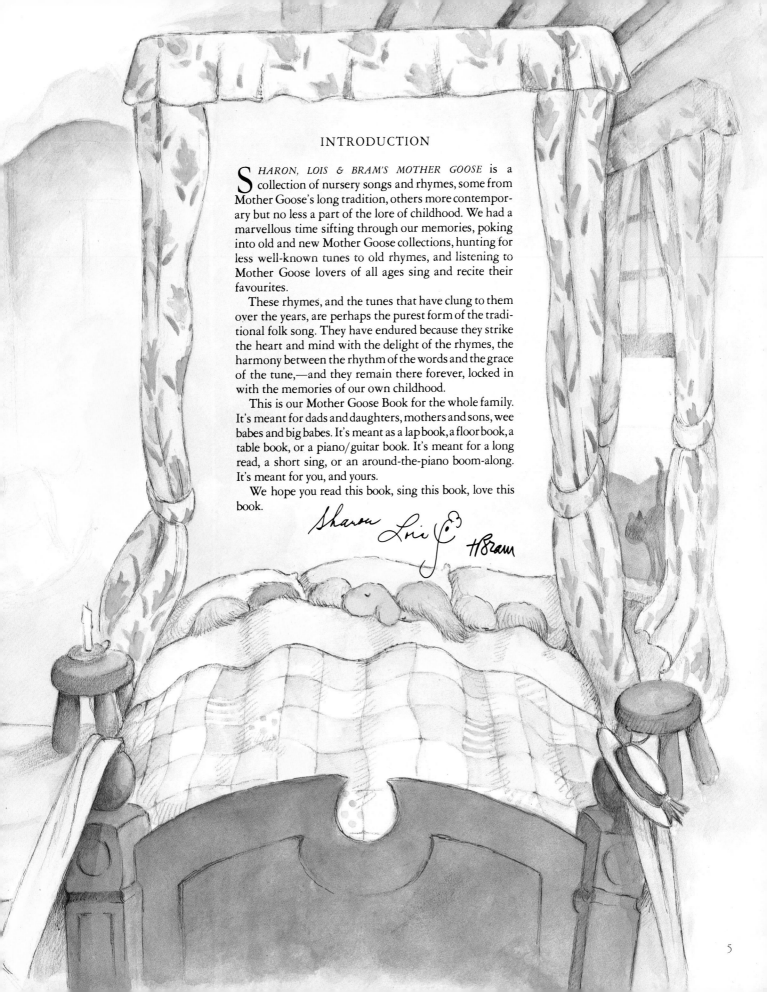

INTRODUCTION

*S*HARON, LOIS & BRAM'S MOTHER GOOSE is a collection of nursery songs and rhymes, some from Mother Goose's long tradition, others more contemporary but no less a part of the lore of childhood. We had a marvellous time sifting through our memories, poking into old and new Mother Goose collections, hunting for less well-known tunes to old rhymes, and listening to Mother Goose lovers of all ages sing and recite their favourites.

These rhymes, and the tunes that have clung to them over the years, are perhaps the purest form of the traditional folk song. They have endured because they strike the heart and mind with the delight of the rhymes, the harmony between the rhythm of the words and the grace of the tune,—and they remain there forever, locked in with the memories of our own childhood.

This is our Mother Goose Book for the whole family. It's meant for dads and daughters, mothers and sons, wee babes and big babes. It's meant as a lap book, a floor book, a table book, or a piano/guitar book. It's meant for a long read, a short sing, or an around-the-piano boom-along. It's meant for you, and yours.

We hope you read this book, sing this book, love this book.

Sharon Lois H Bram

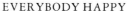
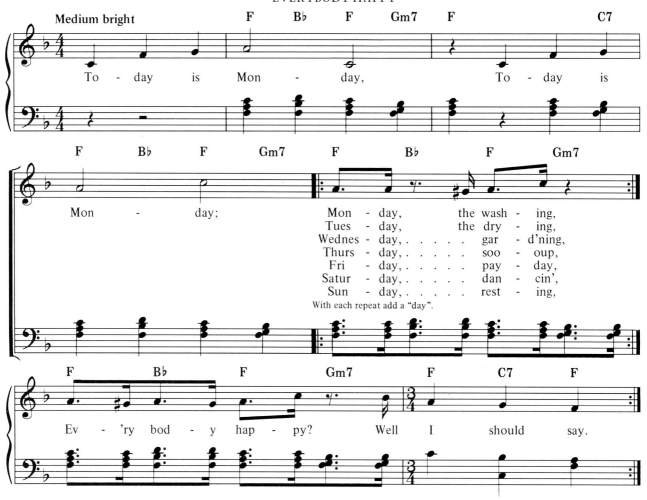

Medium bright

F   Bb   F   Gm7   F   C7

To - day   is   Mon - day,   To - day   is

F   Bb   F   Gm7   F   Bb   F   Gm7

Mon - day;

Mon - day,	the wash - ing,
Tues - day,	the dry - ing,
Wednes - day,	gar - d'ning,
Thurs - day,	soo - oup,
Fri - day,	pay - day,
Satur - day,	dan - cin',
Sun - day,	rest - ing,

With each repeat add a "day".

F   Bb   F   Gm7   F   C7   F

Ev - 'ry bod - y hap - py?   Well   I   should   say.

Today is Tuesday,
Today is Tuesday;
  Tuesday, the drying,
  Everybody happy?
  Well, I should say.

Today is Wednesday,
Today is Wednesday;
  Wednesday, the gardening,
  Everybody happy?
  Well, I should say.

Today is Thursday,
Today is Thursday;
  Thursday, soo-oup,
  Everybody happy?
  Well, I should say.

Today is Friday,
Today is Friday;
  Friday, payday,
  Everybody happy?
  Well, I should say.

Today is Saturday,
Today is Saturday;
  Saturday, dancing,
  Everybody happy?
  Well, I should say.

Today is Sunday,
Today is Sunday;
  Sunday, resting,
  Everybody happy?
  Well, I should say.

LAZY MARY

Brightly

La - zy Mar - y, will you get up, Will you get up, will you get up?

La - zy Mar - y, will you get up, So ear - ly in the morn - ing.

Oh, no, dear mother, I won't get up,
Won't get up, won't get up.
No, dear mother, I won't get up
So early in the morning.

Lightly and brightly

Blue - bird, blue - bird, through my win - dow, Blue - bird, blue - bird, through my win - dow,

Blue - bird, blue - bird, through my win - dow, Oh! John - nie, aren't you tired?

Find a lit - tle friend and tap him on the shoul - der, Find a lit - tle friend and tap him on the shoul - der,
(her) (her)

Find a lit - tle friend and tap him on the shoul - der, Oh! John - nie, aren't you tired?
(her)

9

There was a little man

And he had a little crumb,

And over the mountain he did run.

With a belly full of fat

And a big tall hat,

And a pancake stuck to his bum, bum, bum.

There was a little man
And he had a little crumb,
And over the mountain
He did run.

With a belly full of fat
And a big tall hat,
And a pancake stuck to his
Bum, bum, bum.

Bird, oh, bird,
    Come under my bonnet,
And you shall have bread
    With honey upon it.
You shall have sugar in coffee and tea,
And play every day with baby and me.

Pease por-ridge hot, Pease por-ridge cold, Pease por-ridge in the pot Nine days old.

Some like it hot, Some like it cold, Some like it in the pot Nine days old.

First clap baby's hands together,

Clap!

then pat baby's cheeks (or yours).

Keep claps going in time with the rhyme.

Mix a pancake,
Stir a pancake,
Pop it in the pan.

Fry a pancake,
Toss a pancake,
Catch it if you can.

Do the actions with the words.

HEAD AND SHOULDERS

To the tune of London Bridge

Head and shoulders, knees and toes,
  Knees and toes, knees and toes;
Head and shoulders, knees and toes,
  Eyes, ears, mouth and nose.

Tête, épaules, genoux et pieds,
  Genoux et pieds, genoux et pieds;
Tête, épaules, genoux et pieds,
  Les yeux, les oreilles, la bouche, le nez.

Brow brinky,
Eye winky,
Chin choppy,
Cheek cherry,
Mouth merry.

PHOEBE IN HER PETTICOAT

Johnny in a coat of blue,
Phoebe in her gown,
Baby in the ponycart
Going down to town.

13

Skip around in a circle on first verse.

MULBERRY BUSH

To the tune of Lazy Mary

Here we go round the mulberry bush,
The mulberry bush, the mulberry bush,
Here we go round the mulberry bush
On a cold and frosty morning.

This is the way we wash our hands,
Wash our hands, wash our hands,
This is the way we wash our hands
On a cold and frosty morning.

This is the way we brush our teeth,
Brush our teeth, brush our teeth,
This is the way we brush our teeth
On a cold and frosty morning.

This is the way we comb our hair,
Comb our hair, comb our hair,
This is the way we comb our hair
On a cold and frosty morning.

This is the way we go to school,
Go to school, go to school,
This is the way we go to school
On a cold and frosty morning.

Mime actions for other verses, then make up your own!

14

If you step on a crack,
You'll marry a Jack.
If you step on a square,
You'll marry a bear.

This is the way the ladies ride,
  Trit, trot, trit, trot.
This is the way the gentlemen ride,
  Jiggety-jog, jiggety-jog.
This is the way the farmers ride,
  Hobblety-hoy, hobblety-hoy.
This is the way the hunters ride,
  Gallopy, gallopy, gallopy
  Over the fence.

Bounce your little one on your knee. Make each
ride different and speed up on "gallopy's"
until the child falls backward onto your leg
on "over the fence."

15

And everywhere that Mary went,
Mary went, Mary went.
And everywhere that Mary went
The lamb was sure to go.

It followed her to school one day,
School one day, school one day.
It followed her to school one day
Which was against the rule.

It made the children laugh and play,
Laugh and play, laugh and play.
It made the children laugh and play
To see a lamb at school.

ABC SONG

To the tune of Twinkle, Twinkle, Little Star

A, B, C, D, E, F, G,
H, I, J, K, L-M-N-O-P,
Q, R, S and T, U, V,
W, X, and Y, and Z.
Now I know my ABC's,
Next time won't you sing with me.

Great A, little a,
   Bouncing B,
The cat's in the cupboard
   And can't see me.

Onery, twoery,
Ziccary zan,
Hollow-bone, crack-a-bone,
Ninery, ten.
Spit, spot,
It must be done,
Twiddlum, twaddlum,
Twenty-one.

17

I have ten little fingers
And they all belong to me.
I can make them do things,
Would you like to see?
I can shut them up tight,
I can open them wide,
I can put them together,
And I can make them hide.
I can make them jump high,
I can make them jump low,
I can rolly them around
And fold them just so.

Open, shut them,
Open, shut them,
  Give your hands a clap.
Open, shut them,
Open, shut them,
  Put them in your lap.

WHERE IS THUMBKIN?

Where is pointer, where is pointer?
Here I am, here I am.
How are you this morning?
Very well, I thank you.
Run and hide, run and hide.

Where is middle ma'am, where is middle ma'am?
Here I am, here I am.
How are you this morning?
Very well, I thank you.
Run and hide, run and hide.

Where is ring man, where is ring man?
Here I am, here I am.
How are you this morning?
Very well, I thank you.
Run and hide, run and hide.

Where is pinky, where is pinky?
Here I am, here I am.
How are you this morning?
Very well, I thank you.
Run and hide, run and hide.

Where's the whole family, where's the whole family?
Here we are, here we are.
How are you this morning?
Very well, we thank you.
Run and hide, run and hide.

WHAT SHALL WE DO WHEN WE ALL GO OUT?

Lightly - Moderato

What shall we do when we all go out, All go out, All go out, What shall we do when we all go out, When we all go out to play?

We will ride our three-wheel bikes,
  Three-wheel bikes, three-wheel bikes,
We will ride our three-wheel bikes
  When we all go out to play.

We will skate on our roller skates,
  Roller skates, roller skates,
We will skate on our roller skates
  When we all go out to play.

We will see-saw up and down,
  Up and down, up and down,
We will see-saw up and down
  When we all go out to play.

One for the money,
Two for the show,
Three to make ready,
And four to go!

RING-A-RING O' ROSES

Ring - a-ring o' ro - ses, a pock - et full of po - sies,

Hush - a! Hush - a! We all fall down.

The king has sent his daughter
To fetch a pail of water,
  Hush-a! Hush-a!
  All bow down.

The bird upon the steeple
Sits high above the people,
  Hush-a! Hush-a!
  All kneel down.

The wedding bells are ringing,
The boys and girls are singing,
  Hush-a! Hush-a!
  All fall down.

21

FIVE LITTLE CHICKADEES

Bright Calypso

G   Am   D7

Five lit-tle chick-a-dees sit-ting on the floor, One flew a-way and

Am   G   Am

then there were four. Chick-a-dee, chick-a-dee, hap-py and gay,

D7   1 to 4 Am G   5. Am G

Chick-a-dee, chick-a-dee, fly a-way.   fly a-way.

Four little chickadees sitting in a tree,
One flew away and then there were three.
Chickadee, chickadee, happy and gay,
Chickadee, chickadee, fly away.

Three little chickadees don't know what to do,
One flew away and then there were two.
Chickadee, chickadee, happy and gay,
Chickadee, chickadee, fly away.

Two little chickadees not having any fun,
One flew away and then there was one.
Chickadee, chickadee, happy and gay,
Chickadee, chickadee, fly away.

One little chickadee sitting in the sun,
One flew away and then there were none.
Chickadee, chickadee, happy and gay,
Chickadee, chickadee, fly away.

SALLY GO ROUND THE SUN

Sal - ly go round the sun, Sal - ly go round the moon,
Sal - ly go round the chim - ney tops Ev - 'ry af - ter - noon. *Boom!*

LITTLE SALLY SAUCER

Lit - tle Sal - ly Sau - cer, Sit - ting in the wa - ter,
Rise, Sal - ly, rise, Wipe off your eyes, Point to the east, and
point to the west, And point to the ve - ry one That you love the BEST!

23

Build it up with iron bars,
  Iron bars, iron bars;
Build it up with iron bars,
  My fair lady.

Iron bars will bend and break,
  Bend and break, bend and break;
Iron bars will bend and break,
  My fair lady.

Build it up with silver and gold,
  Silver and gold, silver and gold;
Build it up with silver and gold,
  My fair lady.

Silver and gold I've not got,
  I've not got, I've not got;
Silver and gold I've not got,
  My fair lady.

Here's a prisoner I have got,
  I have got, I have got;
Here's a prisoner I have got,
  My fair lady.

Here am I,
Little Jumping Joan;
When nobody's with me,
I'm all alone.

With the index finger of one hand touch the tips of little finger,
ring man, middle man, and index finger of other.

Johnny, Johnny, Johnny, Johnny,
Whoops, Johnny!
Whoops, Johnny!
Johnny, Johnny, Johnny.

JACK AND JILL

Jack and Jill went up the hill To fetch a pail of wa - ter;

Jack fell down and broke his crown, and Jill came tum - bling af - ter.

Walk fingers from toes to knees to climb hill. One hand hangs
on floor for "Jack fell down," the other bangs for "broke his crown."

...roll both hands for "Jill came tumbling after."

Up Jack got and home did trot
As fast as he could caper;
Went to bed and bound his head
With vinegar and brown paper.

the first "Whoops, Johnny!" slide from the tip of pointer to the tip of thumb. On the second "Whoops, Johnny!" slide from tip of thumb to tip of pointer.

Touch the tips of middle man, ringman and index finger.

Humpty Dumpty sat on a wall,
Humpty Dumpty had a great fall;
All the King's horses and all the King's men
Couldn't put Humpty together again.

Humpty Dumpty sat on a wall,
Eating black bananas.
Where do you think he put the skins?
Down the King's pajamas.

Place a small piece of moistened paper on the nail of each index finger.

On "Fly away, Peter!" fly one hand behind your back and substitute the middle finger for the index finger.

Return that hand right away to face your audience. Repeat this action with the other hand for "Fly away Paul!"

Reverse the whole procedure for "Come back Peter! Come back Paul!"

Two little blackbirds
Sitting on a wall;
One named Peter,
The other named Paul.
Fly away, Peter!
Fly away, Paul!
Come back, Peter!
Come back, Paul!

Bright March

THE GRAND OLD DUKE OF YORK

Oh, the grand old Duke of York, He had ten thou - sand men; He marched them up to the top of the hill And he marched them down a - gain. And when they were up, they were up, And when they were down they were down, And when they were on - ly half - way up They were nei - ther up nor down.

29

Baby and I
Were baked in a pie,
The gravy was wonderful hot.

We had nothing to pay
To the baker that day,
And so we crept out of the pot.

RIG-A-JIG-JIG

Medium bright

C   G7   C

As I was walk-ing down the street, Down the street, down the street, A

G7   C

pret-ty girl I chanced to meet, Heigh-ho, Heigh-ho, heigh-ho.

Chorus

C   (C♯°)   G7   C

Rig-a-jig-jig and a-way we go, A-way we go, a-way we go,

C   G7   C

Rig-a-jig-jig and a-way we go, Heigh-ho, heigh-ho, heigh-ho.

Smiling girls, rosy boys,
Come and buy my little toys;
Monkeys made of gingerbread
And sugar horses painted red.

MY PONY BOY

Pony Boy, Pony Boy, Won't you be my Pony Boy? Don't say no, Here we go,

Right across the plain. Mar-ry me, car-ry me, Ride a-way with you.

Gid-di-up, Gid-di-up, Gid-di-up, Whoa! My Po-ny Boy.

Ride a cock-horse to Banbury Cross
To see a fine lady upon a white horse;
Rings on her fingers and bells on her toes,
And she shall have music wherever she goes.

RINGS ON HER FINGERS

Brightly

For she's got rings on her fin-gers, Bells on her

toes; El-e-phants to ride u-pon, My lit-tle Ir-ish

rose. So come to her par-ty Up-on Saint Pat-rick's

day; She's Mis-tress Jim-bo, Jum-bo, Jid-di-boo Jay O' Shea!

(Verse 1)

He promised he'd buy me a fairing should please me,
And then for a kiss, oh! he vowed he would tease me,
He promised he'd bring me a bunch of blue ribbons
To tie up my bonny brown hair.

Moderato

Chorus Oh, dear! What can the mat-ter be? Dear,

dear! What can the mat-ter be? Oh, dear!

What can the mat-ter be? John-nie's so long at the fair.

34

Verse 2 He prom-ised to bring me a bas-ket of po-sies, A gar-land of li-lies, A gar-land of ros-es, A lit-tle straw hat to set off the blue rib-bons That tie up my bon-ny brown hair. And it's

D.C. al Fine

35

Marcia - moderato

Sol - dier, sol - dier, won't you mar - ry me, With your mus - ket, fife and drum? Oh, how can I mar - ry such a pret - ty maid as thee, When I have no coat to put on? So on.

So off she ran to the clothier's shop
Just as fast as she could run,
And she bought him a coat of the very, very best,
And the soldier put it on.

Soldier, soldier, won't you marry me,
With your musket, fife and drum?
Oh, how can I marry such a pretty maid as thee,
When I have no pants to put on?

So off she ran to the tailor's shop
Just as fast as she could run,
And she bought him some pants of the very, very best,
And the soldier put them on.

Soldier, soldier, won't you marry me,
With your musket, fife and drum?
Oh, how can I marry such a pretty maid as thee,
When I have no boots to put on?

So off she ran to the cobbler's shop
    Just as fast as she could run,
And she bought him some boots of the very, very best,
    And the soldier put them on.

Soldier, soldier, won't you marry me,
    With your musket, fife and drum?
Oh, how can I marry such a pretty maid as thee,
    When I have no hat to put on?

So off she ran to the hatter's shop
    Just as fast as she could run,
And she bought him a hat of the very, very best,
    And the soldier put it on.

Soldier, soldier, won't you marry me,
    With your musket, fife and drum?
Well, how can I marry such a pretty maid as thee . . .
    With a wife and children at home!

One thing at a time,
    And that done well,
Is a very good rule,
    As many can tell.

37

Georgie Porgie, pudding and pie,
Kissed the girls and made them cry;
When the boys came out to play,
Georgie Porgie ran away.

BOBBY SHAFTO

Slowly - quasi rubato

Bob - by Shaf - to's gone to sea, Sil - ver buck - les on his knee;

He'll come back and mar - ry me. Bon - ny Bob - by Shaf - to.

Bobby Shafto's fat and fair,
Combing down his yellow hair;
He's my love for evermore,
Bonny Bobby Shafto!

OLD·KING COLE

Old King Cole was a merry old soul,
And a merry old soul was he;
   He called for his pipe,
    And he called for his bowl,
And he called for his clarinets three.

Every clarinetist had a fine clarinet,
And a fine clarinet had he;
   There's none so rare
    As can compare
With King Cole and his clarinets three.

Old King Cole was a merry old soul,
And a merry old soul was he;
   He called for his pipe,
    And he called for his bowl,
And he called for his trumpeters three.

Every trumpeter had a fine trumpet,
And a very fine trumpet had he;
   There's none so rare
    As can compare
With King Cole and his trumpeters three.

Old King Cole was a merry old soul,
And a merry old soul was he;
   He called for his pipe,
    And he called for his bowl,
And he called for his drummers three.

Every drummer had a fine drum,
And a very fine drum had he;
   There's none so rare
    As can compare
With King Cole and his drummers three.

I had a little husband, no bigger than my thumb;
I put him in a pint pot and there I bade him drum.
I gave him some garters to garter up his hose,
And a little silk handkerchief to wipe his pretty nose.

Handy Pandy, Jack-a-dandy,
Loves plum cake and sugar candy.
He bought some at the grocer's shop
And out he came, hop, hop, hop!

Hippity hop to the barber shop
To buy a stick of candy;
  One for you,
  One for me,
One for Sister Sandy.

Five brown buns in a bakery shop,
Five brown buns with the
  sugar on the top;
Along came a man with a
  penny in his hand,
He took one bun...
And away he ran.

Four brown buns in a bakery shop,
Four brown buns with the
  sugar on the top;
Along came a man with a
  penny in his hand,
He took one bun...
And away he ran.

Three brown buns in a bakery shop,
Three brown buns with the
  sugar on the top;
Along came a man with a
  penny in his hand,
He took one bun...
And away he ran.

42

Two brown buns in a bakery shop,
Two brown buns with the
  sugar on the top;
Along came a man with a
  penny in his hand,
He took one bun...
And away he ran.

One brown bun in a bakery shop,
One brown bun with the
  sugar on the top;
Along came a man with a
  penny in his hand,
He took one bun...
And away he ran.

(Sadly and slowly.)

No brown buns in a bakery shop,
No brown buns with the
  sugar on the top;
Along came a man with a
  penny in his hand,
He took one look...
And away he ran!

Hold up five fingers of one hand and wave from side to side.

Sprinkle sugar with the other hand.

March your thumb from the side of your body to the buns.

Take off one bun.

Then "hide" it behind your back.

43

TO MARKET

To mar - ket, to mar - ket, to buy a fat pig;

Home a - gain, home a - gain, Jig - ge - ty jig. To mar - ket, to mar - ket, to

buy a fat hog; Home a - gain, home a - gain, Jig - ge - ty jog.

TOM, TOM, THE PIPER'S SON

Tom, Tom, the pi - per's son, Stole a pig and a - way he run; The

pig was eat, And Tom was beat, And Tom went howl - ing down the street.

This little piggy went to market,
This little piggy stayed home,
This little piggy ate roast beef,
This little piggy had none,
And this little piggy cried,
Wee-wee-wee-wee-wee,
All the way home.

This little pig had a rub-a-dub,
This little pig had a scrub-a-scrub,
This little pig-a-wig ran upstairs,
This little pig-a-wig called out, Bears!
Down came the jar with a loud
Slam! Slam!
And this little pig had all the jam.

Peter Piper picked a peck of pickled peppers;
A peck of pickled peppers Peter Piper picked.
If Peter Piper picked a peck of pickled peppers,
Where's the peck of pickled peppers Peter Piper picked?

Cobbler, cobbler, mend my shoe,
Get it done by half-past two;
Half-past two is much too late,
Get it done by half-past eight.

Cobbler, cobbler, mend my shoe,
Give it a stitch and that will do;
Here's a nail and there's a prod,
And now my shoe is quite well shod.

I've no time to sit and sigh,
 No patience to wait till time goes by,
So kiss me quick, I'm off, good-bye —
 Pop! Goes the weasel.

HIGGLETY, PIGGLETY POP

Moderato - staccato

Higglety, Pigglety, pop! The dog has eaten the mop. The pig's in a hurry, The cat's in a flurry, Higglety, Pigglety, pop!

Dickery, dickery, dare,
The pig flew up in the air;
The man in brown
Soon brought him down,
Dickery, dickery, dare.

48

BOW-WOW, says the dog;
MEW-MEW, says the cat;
GRUNT-GRUNT, goes the hog;
And SQUEAK, says the rat.
TU-WHO, says the owl;
CAW-CAW, goes the crow;
QUACK-QUACK, goes the duck,
And MOO, says the cow.

Wouldn't it be funny?
Wouldn't it, now?
If the dog said, MOO-OO
And the cow said, BOW-WOW?
If the cat sang and whistled,
And the bird said, MIAW-OW?
Wouldn't it be funny?
Wouldn't it, now?

To scratch where it itches
Is better than fine clothes or riches.

Slowly and sweetly

I know a lit-tle puss-y, I see her ev-'ry day; She lives out in the mead-ow, She nev-er runs a-way. She'll al-ways be a puss-y, She'll nev-er be a cat; Her name is Puss-y Wil-low, Now what do you think of that? Meow, meow, meow, meow, meow, Meow, meow, meow, Scat, cat!

Six little mice sat down to spin;
Pussy passed by and she peeped in.
What are you doing, my little men?
Weaving coats for gentlemen.
Shall I come in and cut off your threads?
No, no, Mistress Pussy, you'd bite off our heads.
Oh, no, I'll not; I'll help you to spin.
That may be so, but you don't come in.

THREE BLIND MICE

Three blind mice, Three blind mice, See how they run,

see how they run; They all ran af - ter the farm - er's wife, She cut off their tails with a

carv - ing knife; Did you ev - er see such a sight in your life as Three blind mice?

Wiggle two fingers of one hand in the palm of the other hand.

Make the caterpillar crawl along your arm to your shoulder.

ARABELLA MILLER

To the tune of Twinkle, Twinkle, Little Star

Little Arabella Miller
Had a fuzzy caterpillar.
First it climbed upon her mother,
Then upon her baby brother.
They said, Arabella Miller,
Put away your caterpillar!

Little Arabella Miller
Had a fuzzy caterpillar.
First it climbed upon her mother,
Then upon her baby brother.
They said, Arabella Miller,
How we love your caterpillar!

Take two fingers of the other hand and crawl them up the other arm to the other shoulder.

Make both caterpillars crawl up the sides of your face.

Put both hands behind your back.

For verse 2, repeat the actions, smiling.
At the end, stroke the caterpillar gently.

Little Miss Muffet
Sat on a tuffet,
Eating her curds and whey;
There came a great spider
And sat down beside her,
And frightened Miss Muffet away.

Five lit - tle speck - led frogs Sit - ting on a speck - led log,

Eat - ing the most de - li - cious flies, Yum, yum. Child's name fell in - to the pool

Where it was so nice and cool, Now there are four green speck - led frogs. Ribbet, Ribbet.

Two little speckled frogs
Sitting on a speckled log,
Eating the most delicious flies.
Yum, yum.
_____ fell into the pool
Where it was so nice and cool;
Now there is one green speckled frog.
Ribbet, ribbet.

One little speckled frog
Sitting on a speckled log,
Eating the most delicious flies.
Yum, yum.
_____ fell into the pool
Where it was so nice and cool;
Now there are no green speckled frogs.
Ribbet, ribbet.

Four little speckled frogs
Sitting on a speckled log,
Eating the most delicious flies.
Yum, yum.
_____ fell into the pool
Where it was so nice and cool;
Now there are three green speckled frogs.
Ribbet, ribbet.

Three little speckled frogs
Sitting on a speckled log,
Eating the most delicious flies.
Yum, yum.
_____ fell into the pool
Where it was so nice and cool;
Now there are two green speckled frogs.
Ribbet, ribbet.

Make swimming motions

Hands behind back

Flutter fingers

Hug yourself as if you're freezing

Point down deep

Look out to sea

Go to sleep

Swimming and diving motions.

Five little fishies
Swimming in the pool,
The first one said,
This pool is cool.
The second one said,
This pool is deep.
The third one said,
I'd like to sleep.
The fourth one said,
Let's swim and dip.
The fifth one said,
I see a ship.
The fisherman's line went
Splish, splish, splash,
(Fast) And away the five
Little fishies dash!

Where ya goin', little boy?
'ishin'.
What ya got in your mouth, little boy?
'Urms.

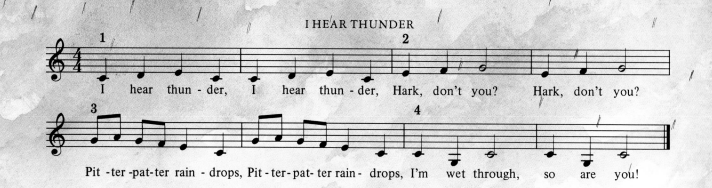

I HEAR THUNDER

1 2

I hear thun-der, I hear thun-der, Hark, don't you? Hark, don't you?

3 4

Pit-ter-pat-ter rain-drops, Pit-ter-pat-ter rain-drops, I'm wet through, so are you!

Drum your feet

Pretend to listen

Make rain with your fingers

Shake your whole body

Point to a neighbour

Rain, rain, go to Spain,
Never show your face again!

Doctor Foster went to Gloucester
In a shower of rain;
He stepped in a puddle
Right up to his middle,
And never went back there again.

ONE MISTY, MOISTY MORNING

Brightly

One mist-y, moist-y morn-ing, When cloud-y was the weath-er, I chanced to meet an

old man clothed all in leath-er. Clothed all in leath-er from his head up to his

chin, Sing-ing How d'you do, and how d'you do, and how d'you do a-gain.

58

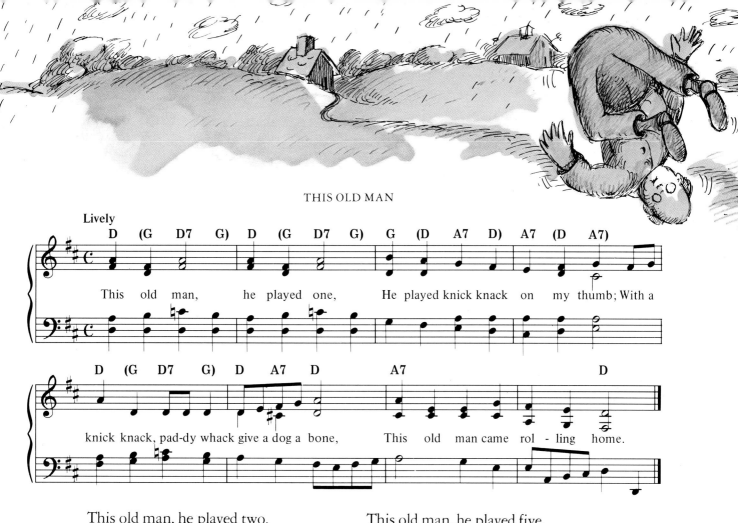

THIS OLD MAN

Lively

This old man, he played one,
He played knick knack on my thumb; With a
knick knack, pad-dy whack give a dog a bone,
This old man came rol - ling home.

This old man, he played two,
He played knick knack on my shoe...

This old man, he played three,
He played knick knack on my knee...

This old man, he played four,
He played knick knack on the floor...

This old man, he played five,
He played knick knack on the hive...

And so on...make up your own rhymes.

Last verse:

This old man, he played ten,
He played knick knack over again...

Show the numbers with your fingers.

Show the parts of the body, the floor, etc.

Knick knack: bang fists twice.

Paddy wack: clap hands twice.

Give the dog a bone: throw a bone.

Rolling home: roll hands around each other.

Rain, rain, go a - way; Come a - gain some
oth - er day; All the chil - dren want to play.

Rain on the green grass,
Rain on the tree,
Rain on the housetop,
But not on me!

The big fat spider
Went up the waterspout;
Down came the rain
And washed the spider out;
Out came the sun
And dried up all the rain;
Then the big fat spider
Went up the spout again.

The teensy weensy spider
Went up the waterspout;
Down came the rain
And washed the spider out;
Out came the sun
And dried up all the rain;
Then the teensy weensy spider
Went up the spout again.

If you want to live and thrive,
Let a spider stay alive.

I'd have it pump some water,
 Some water, some water,
I'd have it pump some water,
 Yes, that is what I would do.

And then I'd have a duck pond,
 A duck pond, a duck pond,
And then I'd have a duck pond,
 Yes, that is what I would do.

The ducks would make their wings flap,
 Their wings flap, their wings flap,
The ducks would make their wings flap,
 Yes, that is what they would do.

If I could have a windmill,
 A windmill, a windmill,
If I could have a windmill,
 I know what I would do.

As I went up in my penny balloon,
My penny balloon went pop;
I fell right down to the deep blue sea,
And caught a fish in my frock.

Terence McDiddler,
The three-stringed fiddler,
Can charm, if you please,
The fish from the seas.

Count the fingers on one hand

Count the fingers on the other hand

Wiggle the little finger at the end

One, two, three-four-five,
Once I caught a fish alive;
Six, seven, eight-nine-ten,
Then I let it go again.

Why did you let it go?
Because it bit my finger so.
Which finger did it bite?
The little finger on the right.

If all the seas were one sea,
What a *great* sea that would be!
If all the trees were one tree,
What a *great* tree that would be!
And if all the axes were one axe,
What a *great* axe that would be!
And if all the men were one man,
What a *great* man that would be!
And if the *great* man took the *great* axe,
And cut down the *great* tree,
And let it fall into the *great* sea,
What a splish-splash that would be!

Swan swam over the sea,
Swim, swan, swim!
Swan swam back again.
Well swum, swan!

ALLEE, ALLEE-O

Moderato - Lightly

Oh the big ship's sail - ing on the Al - lee Al - lee O, The
Al - lee, Al - lee O, the Al - lee, Al - lee O. Oh, the
big ship's sail - ing on the Al - lee, Al - lee O, On the
last day of Sep - tem - ber.

Oh, the big ship's sailing and she's going out to sea,
  Going out to sea, going out to sea;
Oh, the big ship's sailing and she's going out to sea,
  On the last day of September.

Oh, the big ship's sailing on the Allee, Allee-O,
  The Allee, Allee-O, the Allee, Allee-O;
Oh, the big ship's sailing on the Allee, Allee-O,
  On the last day of September.

Medium bright

Pol - ly put the ket - tle on, Pol - ly put the ket - tle on,

Pol - ly put the ket - tle on, We'll all have tea. Su - kie, take it off a - gain,

Su - kie, take it off a - gain, Su - kie, take it off a - gain, They've all gone a - way.

Crosspatch,
Draw the latch,
Sit by the fire and spin;
Take a cup
And drink it up,
Then call your neighbours in.

Hickety, pickety, my black hen,
She lays eggs for gentlemen;
Gentlemen come every day
To see what my black hen doth lay.
Sometimes nine and sometimes ten,
Hickety, pickety, my black hen.

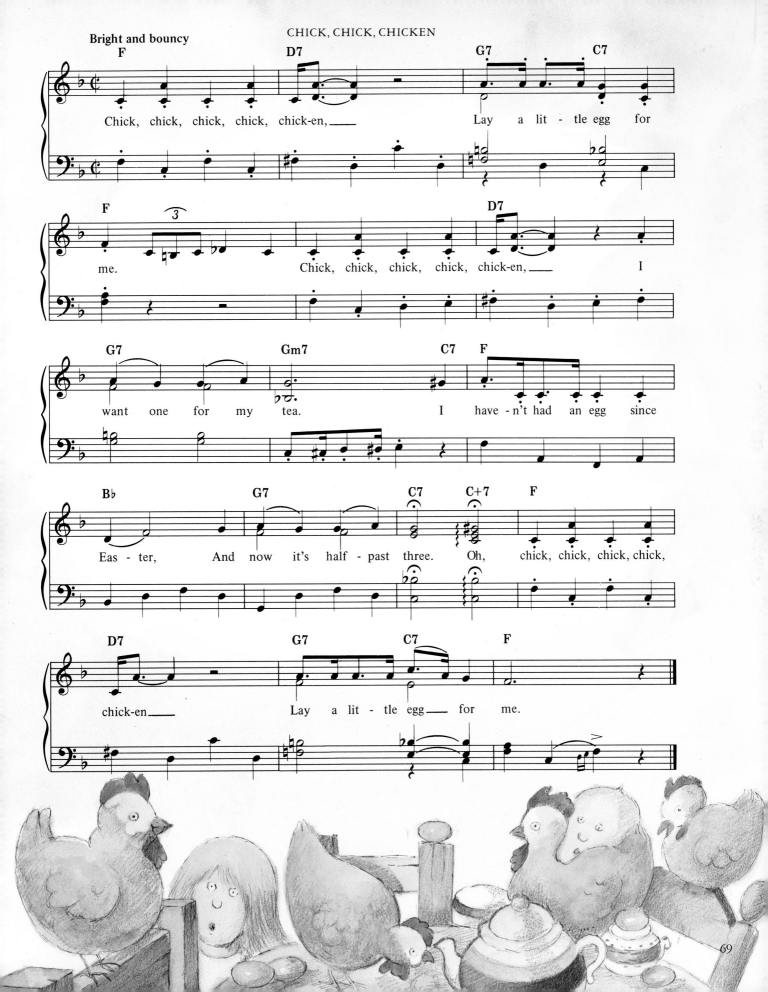

One, one
   Cinnamon bun
Two, two
   Chicken stew
Three, three
   Cakes and tea
Four, four
   I want more
Five, five
   Honey in a hive
Six, six
   Pretzel sticks
Seven, seven
   Straight from heaven
Eight, eight
   Clean your plate
Nine, nine
   Look at mine
Ten, ten
   Start over again!

LITTLE JACK HORNER

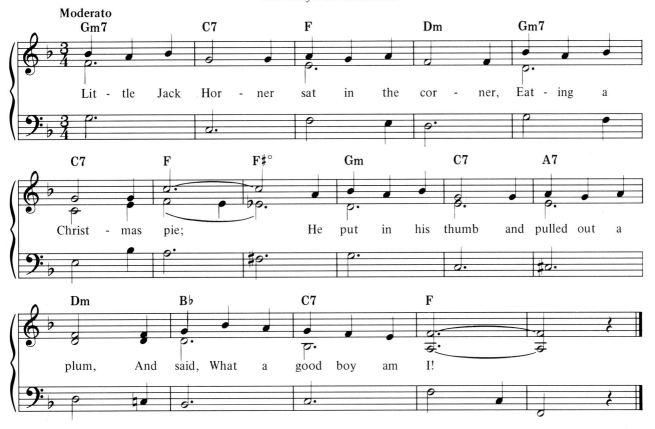

Moderato

Gm7   C7   F   Dm   Gm7

Lit - tle Jack Hor - ner sat in the cor - ner, Eat - ing a

C7   F   F#°   Gm   C7   A7

Christ - mas pie;   He put in his thumb and pulled out a

Dm   Bb   C7   F

plum, And said, What a good boy am I!

When Jack's a very good boy,
He shall have cakes and custard;
But when he does nothing but cry,
He shall have nothing but mustard.

71

Here are the lady's knives and forks,
Here is my lady's table;
Here is the lady's looking glass,
And here is the baby's cradle.

Lace fingers palms up.

Turn palms down.

Raise index fingers, tips touching.

Raise little fingers, tips touching and rock the cradle.

I eat my peas with honey;
I've done it all my life.
It makes the peas taste funny,
But it keeps them on the knife.

One for me and one for you,
If there's one left over then what'll we do?
Take up a knife and cut it in two
So there's one for me and one for you.

Make fist with the thumb tucked inside.

Pop out the thumb,

Lift up the pointer finger, then lift up the other three fingers, one at a time.

Five plump peas in a pea pod pressed,
One grew...
Two grew...
So did all the rest.

They grew...
And they grew...
And they grew and never stopped.
They grew so fat that the pea pod
POPPED!

Both hands face each other.

With arms opening wider and wider.

Clap hands together on "popped!"

Soon as supper's et, Mama hollers,
  Mama hollers, Mama hollers;
Soon as supper's et, Mama hollers,
  Time to go to sleep.

Soon as we touch our head to the pillow,
  Head to the pillow, head to the pillow;
Soon as we touch our head to the pillow,
  Go to sleep right smart.

Soon as the rooster crows in the morning,
  Crows in the morning, crows in the morning;
Soon as the rooster crows in the morning,
  Time to go to school.

Soon as we all cook sweet potatoes,
  Sweet potatoes, sweet potatoes;
Soon as we all cook sweet potatoes,
  Eat 'em right straight up.

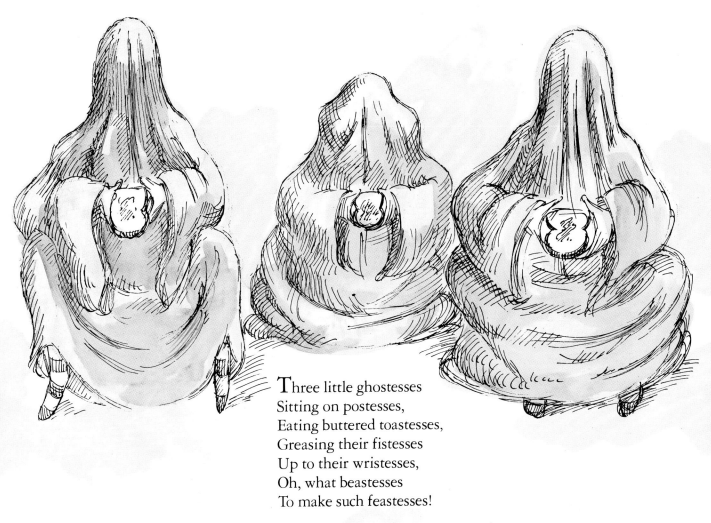

Three little ghostesses
Sitting on postesses,
Eating buttered toastesses,
Greasing their fistesses
Up to their wristesses,
Oh, what beastesses
To make such feastesses!

Davy Davy Dumpling,
Boil him in the pot;
Sugar him and butter him
And eat him while he's hot.

Who's that ringing at my doorbell?
A little pussycat that isn't very well.
Rub its nose in a little mutton fat,
For that's the best cure for a little pussycat.

Of a little take a little,
    Manners so to do;
Of a little leave a little,
    That is manners, too.

I do not like thee, Doctor Fell.
The reason why I cannot tell,
But this I know and know full well,
I do not like thee, Doctor Fell.

MISS POLLY HAD A DOLLY

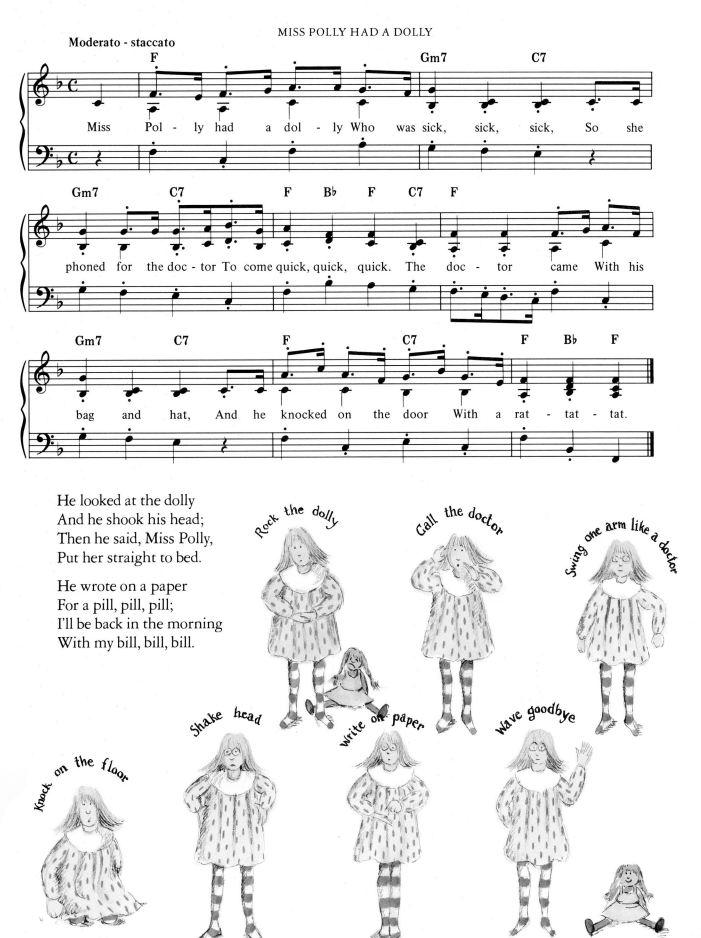

He looked at the dolly
And he shook his head;
Then he said, Miss Polly,
Put her straight to bed.

He wrote on a paper
For a pill, pill, pill;
I'll be back in the morning
With my bill, bill, bill.

Bright and sassy

Miss Lu-cy had a ba-by, His name was Ti-ny Tim; She put him in the bath-tub To see if he could swim. He drank up all the wa-ter, He ate up all the soap, He tried to eat the bath-tub, But it would-n't go down his throat.

Miss Lucy called the doctor,
Miss Lucy called the nurse,
Miss Lucy called the lady
With the alligator purse.

In came the doctor,
In came the nurse,
In came the lady
With the alligator purse.

Measles, said the doctor,
Measles, said the nurse,
Chicken pox, said the lady
With the alligator purse.

Penicillin, said the doctor,
Penicillin, said the nurse,
Pizza, said the lady
With the alligator purse.

Out went the doctor,
Out went the nurse,
Out went the lady
With the alligator purse.

Oh, the cat's got the measles,
The dog's got the flu,
The donkey's got the chicken pox,
And so have YOU!

An apple a day
Sends the doctor away.

Apple in the morning,
Doctor's warning.

Roast apple at night
Starves the doctor outright.

Three each day, seven days a week,
Ruddy apple, ruddy cheek.

Bouncing

Dance to your dad-dy, My lit-tle lad-dy, Dance to your
dad-dy, My lit-tle lamb. You shall have a fish-y In your lit-tle
dish-y, You shall have a fish-y When the boat comes in.

Dance to your mammy,
　My little lamby,
Dance to your mammy,
　My little lamb.
You shall have a fishy
　In your little dishy,
You shall have a fishy
　When the boat comes in.

Bring Daddy home
With a fiddle and a drum,
A pocket full of spices,
An apple and a plum.

Rigadoon, rigadoon,
　Now let him fly;
Sit him on Father's foot,
　Jump him up high.

80

BABY BYE

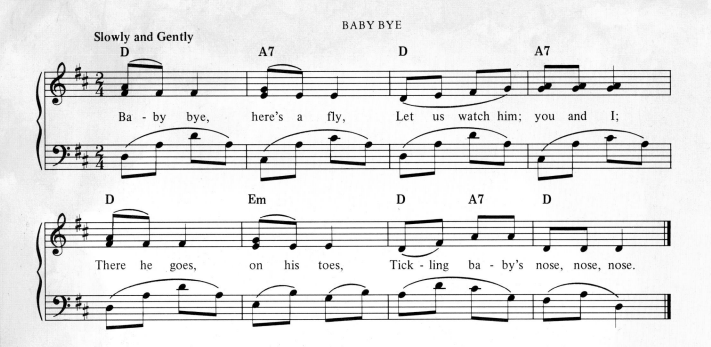

Slowly and Gently

| D | A7 | D | A7 |

Ba - by bye, here's a fly, Let us watch him; you and I;

| D | Em | D | A7 | D |

There he goes, on his toes, Tick - ling ba - by's nose, nose, nose.

Flutter fingers like a fly, then touch baby's nose.

There was a little girl
Who had a little curl
Right in the middle of her forehead.
When she was good
She was very, very good —
But when she was bad she was horrid.

Rub-a-dub-dub, three men in a tub,
And who do you think they be?
The butcher, the baker, the candlestick maker
Turn them out, knaves all three!

Shoe a little horse,
Shoe a little mare,
But let the little coltie
Go bare, bare, bare.

ROW, ROW, ROW YOUR BOAT

Row, row, row your boat Gent-ly down the stream.

Mer-ri-ly, mer-ri-ly, mer-ri-ly, mer-ri-ly, Life is but a dream.

JEREMIAH

Jer-e-mi-ah, blow the fi-ah, Puff, puff, puff.

SPOKEN: First you blow it gently,
Then you blow it rough.

Jer-e-mi-ah, blow the fi-ah, Puff, puff, puff.

Star light, star bright,
The first star I see tonight.
I wish I may, I wish I might,
Have the wish I wish tonight.

There was an old woman tossed up in a basket,
   Seventeen times as high as the moon;
Where she was going I couldn't but ask it,
   For in her hand she carried a broom.

Old woman, old woman, old woman, quoth I,
   Where are you going to up so high?
To brush the cobwebs off the sky!
   May I go with you? Aye, by and by.

Wee Willie Winkie runs through the town,
Upstairs and downstairs in his nightgown;
Rapping at the window, crying through the lock,
   Are the children all in bed?
   For now it's eight o'clock.

When the blazing sun is gone,
When he nothing shines upon,
Then you show your little light,
Twinkle, twinkle, all the night.
Twinkle, twinkle, little star,
How I wonder what you are.

Then the traveller in the dark
Thanks you for your tiny spark,
He could not see where to go
If you did not twinkle so.
Twinkle, twinkle, little star,
How I wonder what you are.

In the dark blue sky you keep,
And often through my curtains peep,
For you never shut your eye
'Til the sun is in the sky.
Twinkle, twinkle, little star,
How I wonder what you are.

As your bright and tiny spark,
Lights one traveller in the dark,
Though I know not what you are,
Twinkle, twinkle, little star.
Twinkle, twinkle, little star,
How I wonder what you are.

Diddle, diddle, dumpling, my son John,
Went to bed with his trousers on;
One shoe off, and one shoe on,
Diddle, diddle, dumpling, my son John.

To bed, to bed,
Says Sleepyhead;
Tarry awhile, says Slow;
Put on the pan,
Says Greedy Nan,
We'll sup before we go.

WHERE'S MY PAJAMAS?

There were ten in the bed, and the lit-tle one said, Roll o - ver, roll

o - ver. So they all rolled o - ver, and one fell out. There were

nine in the bed, and the lit - tle one said, Roll o - ver, roll o - ver.

There were nine in the bed,
And the little one said,
   Roll over, roll over.
So they all rolled over,
   And one fell out.

There were eight in the bed,
And the little one said,
   Roll over, roll over.
So they all rolled over,
   And one fell out.

There were seven in the bed,
And the little one said,
   Roll over, roll over.
So they all rolled over,
   And one fell out.

There were six in the bed,
And the little one said,
   Roll over, roll over.
So they all rolled over,
   And one fell out.

There were five in the bed,
And the little one said,
   Roll over, roll over.
So they all rolled over,
   And one fell out.

There were four in the bed,
And the little one said,
   Roll over, roll over.
So they all rolled over,
   And one fell out.

There were three in the bed,
And the little one said,
   Roll over, roll over.
So they all rolled over,
   And one fell out.

There were two in the bed,
And the little one said,
   Roll over, roll over.
So they all rolled over,
   And one fell out.

There was one in the bed,
And the little one said,

*(To the tune of "He's Got the
Whole World in His Hands")*

I've got the whole mattress to myself,
I've got the whole mattress to myself,
I've got the whole mattress to myself,
   I've got the mattress to myself.

Good night,
Sweet repose.
Half the bed
And all the clothes.

Niddledy, noddledy, to and fro,
Tired and sleepy, to bed we go.
Jump into bed,
Turn out the light,
Head on the pillow,
Shut your eyes tight.

The man in the moon
Looked out of the moon,
And this is what he said,
'Tis time that, now
    I'm getting up,
All babies went to bed.

Go to bed late,
Stay very small.
Go to bed early,
Grow very TALL.

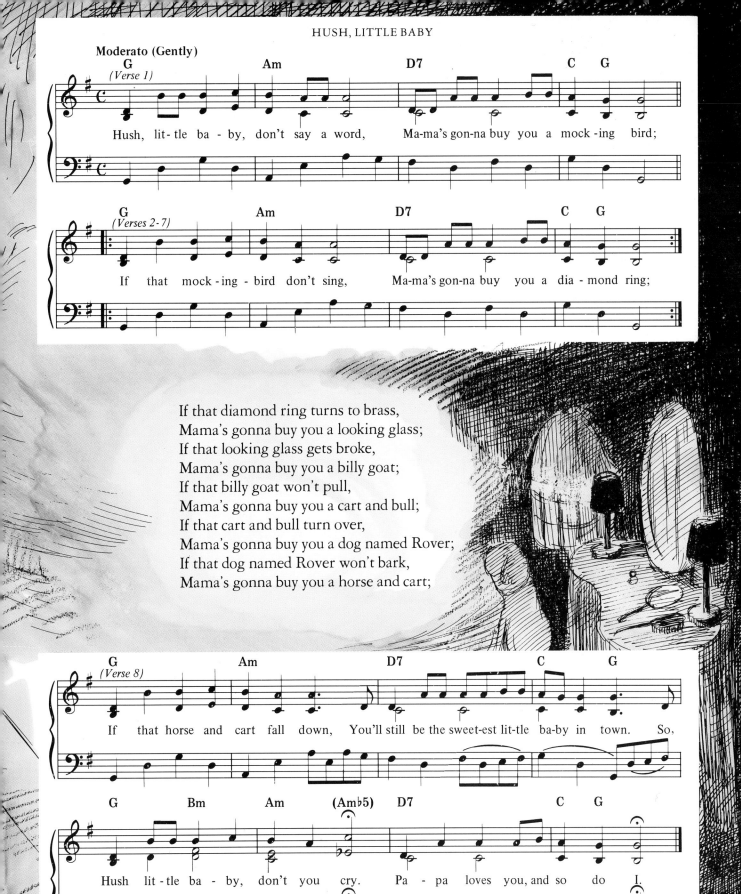

If that diamond ring turns to brass,
Mama's gonna buy you a looking glass;
If that looking glass gets broke,
Mama's gonna buy you a billy goat;
If that billy goat won't pull,
Mama's gonna buy you a cart and bull;
If that cart and bull turn over,
Mama's gonna buy you a dog named Rover;
If that dog named Rover won't bark,
Mama's gonna buy you a horse and cart;

Rock-a-bye, baby,
  Thy cradle is green,
Father's a nobleman,
  Mother's a queen;
And Lizzie's a lady
  And wears a gold ring;
And Johnny's a drummer
  And drums for the king.

Lavender's blue, dilly, dilly,
   Lavender's green;
When I am king, dilly, dilly,
   You'll be my queen.
Who told you so, dilly, dilly,
   Who told you so?
I told myself, dilly, dilly,
   I told me so.

I love to dance, dilly, dilly,
   I love to sing;
When I am queen, dilly, dilly,
   You'll be my king.
Who told you so, dilly, dilly,
   Who told you so?
I told myself, dilly, dilly,
   I told me so.

Hickory, dickory, dock,
The mouse ran up the clock;
The clock struck one,
The mouse ran down;
Hickory, dickory, dock.

One, two, skip a few,
Ninety-nine, a hundred.

Index

They had such enormous fun,
But there were no more elephants
Left to come.